TALES FROM THE DARK SIDE

WALKING
WITH THE
DEAD

Tim Bowler

Illustrated by Jason Cockroft

*Hodder
Children's
Books*

a division of Hodder Headline Limited

CONTENTS

1

THE ALLEYWAY

Two things happened on my fourteenth birthday. I had a massive row with Dad – and I died.

It started around dusk. We were having a week's holiday in Totnes – big mistake. Don't get me wrong. I like Totnes. We often used to go there for little breaks when Dad and Mum were together. It was good to get away from London and we liked to go somewhere different.

And Totnes is different. I don't know what it is about the place. It's like nowhere you've ever been. You feel like you're walking through the present and the past at the same time. We used to go there a lot as a family.

But that was in the days before Mum met Mr Perfect and walked out on us, and then Dad met Angela. Everything's gone wrong since then. It's not that I blame him for going out with someone else. The problem is I don't like her.

She smiles too much and she keeps trying to be matey with me. I wish she wouldn't. And she's got bad skin. I mean, I know it's not her fault and she's always putting cream on and stuff, but she doesn't look good, not the way Mum did.

Anyway, there we were in this grotty guesthouse called Maudlin Lodge. It was in a street that climbed up towards the Kingsbridge Arms, not a part of Totnes I knew at all.

There was no one else staying there – what a surprise – and it was run by this loopy woman called Mrs Capstick. She looked like she had one foot in this world and one foot in some other. And her husband didn't look much better.

We arrived in the late afternoon and within five minutes I was so bored and fed up I wanted to scream.

Then Dad and I had this row. It was all about Angela, of course. She'd bought me this CD collection for my birthday. I suppose she wasn't to know Mum got me the same collection last year, but she should have checked with Dad first.

Anyway, I snapped at her. Dad told me off, so I snapped at him. We let rip at each other for a few minutes. Then I stomped out.

I was fuming. I tramped up the hill, hardly looking where I was going. Yet even in my anger, I could feel something else. Something that should have warned me.

It was a feeling I'd had before, a feeling that I'm walking into trouble and that if I turn away, I can avoid it. Only I never do. It's a pride thing, I suppose. I tell myself I've got a right to go wherever I want.

Like the time I sensed Kenny and his mates were round the corner of the school gym and I had a chance to turn back. Only I went on and there they were. And I got beaten up.

Or the time I knew I shouldn't follow Joel into the camera shop. He hadn't said what he was going to do but I sensed he was going to nick something and probably get caught.

I didn't have to go in with him. I'd even told him I had to get home, and he was OK about it. But I went in. I ignored my hunch, like I always do. Joel got caught, and guess who else got into trouble?

And here was another hunch. It told me to stop and go back to Maudlin Lodge. So of course I carried on up the hill. I thought, why the hell shouldn't I go this way if I want to?

Then I saw this funny little lane to my right. I stopped and looked it over. It was more of an alleyway really, tucked into the pavement. It had high walls on either side and all I could see was a dark passageway dipping for a few yards before twisting away out of sight. What lay beyond I had no idea.

I stared at it. I was still fuming and ready to bite the head off anyone who came by. In fact, I was practically hoping someone would come by so I could do just that. But there was that feeling again. That hunch.

Turn away, it said. Go back to the guesthouse. Make your peace with Dad and Angela.

No way.

I headed down the alleyway with my fists clenched, and before I'd gone more than a few yards I heard the sound of running water.

I stopped and listened. It was so unexpected it was almost magical. I stood there and let it wash over me. Perhaps if I'd stayed there a bit longer, it would have washed away my anger.

But anger doesn't work like that. Not with me anyway. Sometimes I want to hold onto it, and this was one of those times.

I carried on down the alleyway, staring up at the high stone walls on either side. Then suddenly I came out into a sort of triangular yard bordered by walls. Two further alleyways led off it, one climbing on up the hill, the other dipping away to my right.

To my left was the weirdest sight.

2

THE BROKEN BELL

It was some kind of spring or well. But it was like nothing I'd ever seen before. It was quite large and it was roughly rectangular with high stone walls on three sides. The fourth side opened onto the little space where I was standing.

Water trickled out from some point on the far wall but I couldn't see where from. This was partly because the light was fading, but also because my view was blocked by a scruffy old man.

He had his back to me and he was lying in the spring itself. I didn't like the look of him. But he seemed harmless and obviously didn't know I was there. I could creep forward and have a closer look and still have time to run for it if he turned round.

Again I felt that hunch. Turn away. Get out of here. Again I ignored it.

I stole forward until I was just a few feet from the spring. I could see it much more clearly now, even in the dusk.

The base was more or less flat and it had three stone baths, each with a spout above it. I could see water trickling out of one of them.

The floor was covered with stones, many arranged in intricate patterns. On the far wall there was an open grate and a stone ledge with little ornaments that people had left there. I could even see a love-heart made from wood and some words scrawled on it.

But the old man wasn't interested in any of these things. His attention was on a small, dirty-looking object which he had wedged under the running spout and was cleaning as the water splashed onto it.

He appeared to be having some difficulty holding it in place and the water was splashing over him too. But he seemed unconcerned about this. All he cared about was cleaning the thing, whatever it was.

I looked him over. He was certainly a freaky character. He had a long coat with a hood, though this was down over the back of his neck, and the whole thing was so sodden it clung to him.

I could see the outline of a gaunt, wasted body underneath. His hair was scrawny and unkempt, and as wet as the rest of him. I couldn't see his face at all.

Then he turned and I saw a revolting sight. If Angela's skin was bad, this man's was a thousand times worse.

His face was covered in sores. But that wasn't all. His eyes were sunken. His forehead was unnaturally high. He had no teeth.

He was hideous.

He squinted up at me, then spoke in a high, quavering voice.

'Who's that?'

'None of your business,' I said.

'Eh?'

'None of your business!'

He sniffed.

'Friendly type,' he muttered.

I said nothing. He went on squinting up at me. It was obvious he was half-blind as well as half-deaf. I stared back at him, determined to show no fear.

'So you haven't got a name?' he said.

'I've got a name,' I answered. 'But I'm not telling you what it is.'

The man took the object he was washing away from the spout and rested it on the floor behind him. I tried again to make out what it was but the man's body blocked it. He twisted himself painfully round.

I found the look in his eyes unsettling but I managed to glare back at him.

'My name's Stevie,' I said.

I don't know why I told him. I suppose it was just defiance. The old man sniffed again.

'Ah,' he mused. 'Stephen.'

'Not Stephen!' I snapped. 'Stevie!'

'There was a Stephen in the Bible,' the old man went on, in the same musing voice. 'They stoned him to death.'

I felt suddenly cold. The old man moved and I took a step back. He looked up at me.

'Help me stand up, Stephen.'

I kept well back. I wasn't going near this guy.

I saw a hand reaching towards me.

'I need your help, Stephen.'

'Get away from me!'

'Please, Stephen.'

'No!' I stared at him with revulsion. 'You got in by yourself. You can get out by yourself.'

The old man's hand stretched closer. I looked down at it and recoiled.

He had no fingers.

'Get away!' I shouted. 'You're disgusting!'

He drew his hand back without a word. I watched in horror as he tried to push himself up from the floor of the spring. I could see even from here that the other hand was fingerless too.

I looked quickly down at his feet. They were bare – and toeless.

I felt another wave of revulsion.

The old man struggled to his feet. I shouted at him, trying to sound more confident than I felt.

'You see? You didn't need my help at all!'

The old man stood there, swaying. I could hear the heavy sound of his breathing against the trickle of the water. He was watching me again but it was hard to see his expression now that darkness was closing around us.

He lurched towards the edge of the spring. I took a few steps towards the alleyway I had come down.

But the old man had no further interest in me. He struggled out of the spring and stood there for a moment. Then, without a glance in my direction, he shuffled off towards the alleyway that led down the hill.

A moment later he was gone.

I breathed out with relief. He might not have been dangerous but he was creepy. I turned to run back to the guesthouse, then suddenly noticed that the object the old man had been washing was still in the spring. I jumped down and picked it up.

It was a small metal bell.

I shook it but no sound came out. It appeared to be broken.

I glanced over my shoulder for the old man. There was no sign of him. I held the bell up. Even in the darkness it gave off a dull glint. I climbed out of the spring and stood there, kicking some of the water from my shoes.

Then I felt another hunch. A really strong one.

Put the bell down, it said. Leave it where it was.

I gripped it tightly in my hand.

Put it down. Walk away. Do it now.

I squeezed the bell more tightly than ever and set off with it up the alleyway.

As I did so, something cold brushed against my legs.

I shivered and looked down.

There was nothing there. Just water dripping from my trousers onto the stony ground. I walked on and this time felt nothing more.

But something was wrong; and I needed no hunch to tell me what it was.

I was being followed.

3

BIRTHDAY PRESENCE

I could see nothing. Yet I knew something was there.

I walked to the end of the alleyway and set off down the hill towards Maudlin Lodge. It was still following me, whatever it was. I could feel it.

I stopped and looked back through the darkness. All I saw was the pavement, the parked cars, the houses, the streetlamps. Maybe the thing was gone.

Then it brushed against my legs again.

I was shivering with fear now. I looked frantically about me, trying to see what had touched me. A figure appeared in the darkness.

I stiffened.

But it was only Dad.

'Stevie!' he called.

I ran down to him, keeping the bell hidden behind my back.

'Where have you been?' he said.

I looked away. I didn't want to talk about this. I didn't want him to see the bell. And I didn't want him to see I was scared.

'Listen,' said Dad. 'I'm not going to shout at you, OK? I just want us all to get on.'

I said nothing. All I could think about was the spooky presence. It was still close. I could sense it.

'Stevie?' said Dad. 'Are you OK?'

I forced myself to look at him.

'I'm fine. Can we go back to the guesthouse?'

'Sure, but listen.' Dad frowned. 'Can you try and make this work? It's really hard for Angela. And she's doing her best.'

I felt the icy presence brush past my legs again.

'Stevie, you look really jumpy.'

'I'm all right. Can we go back?'

'OK.'

We set off down the hill. Dad still hadn't noticed the bell and I was glad of that. The last thing I wanted was questions right now. I turned it upside down, wedged the handle inside my belt and let my shirt fall over it.

We didn't speak again till we came to Maudlin Lodge. Dad stopped on the doorstep and turned to face me.

'Stevie?'

'Yeah?'

'I just want you to be happy. Especially today. It's your birthday. It's no big deal about the CDs.

We can change them
for something else.'

I tried to look at him but my eyes were racing
everywhere. The icy presence was still close. As
I entered the house, I felt it enter with me.

I stood in the hall, staring about me. Nothing
moved except the pendulum of the grandfather
clock. Then I saw Angela coming down the
stairs.

'Stevie!' she said brightly. 'Did you have a
good walk?'

'I didn't go for a walk,' I answered. 'I went
out to get away from you two.'

'Stevie,' warned Dad.

'Yes, thank you,' I said. 'I had a good walk.'

She joined us in the hall.

'Are you hungry?' she said.

'I suppose.'

'I certainly am. Ah, here's Mrs Capstick.'

I groaned inwardly. That was all I needed. The woman shambled towards us with a disapproving look on her face.

'I've been holding supper for you,' she said coldly.

'Yes, I'm so sorry,' said Dad. 'We'll come along right now.'

'That would be very helpful.'

And she led us through to the dining room. Dinner was a disaster, made even worse by

Dad and Angela's desperate attempts to turn it into a birthday celebration. I wasn't feeling remotely birthday-like.

I was worried about the old man. I was worried about what I'd seen and done. I was worried about the bell hidden under my shirt. I was worried about this unseen presence that kept brushing against my legs.

And now there was something else.

I could feel itching all over my body, especially inside my nose.

'You look really tired, Stevie,' said Dad as we finished our dessert.

I wasn't tired. I was scared, really scared. Something horrible was happening to me and I didn't know what it was. The icy presence brushed against my legs again.

'I hope,' said Dad with a flourish, 'you're not too tired for this!'

He pointed towards the kitchen door and there was Mr Capstick walking forward with a chocolate cake, candles burning on top.

'Wow!' said Angela.

I had the feeling I was supposed to have said that. Mr Capstick put down the cake.

'Wow!' said Dad.

That was definitely my cue.

'Wow!' I said.

And everyone relaxed.

Everyone except me. I felt as wound-up as a spring. Somehow I hid it from them. I blew out the candles. I ate lots of the cake. I told them I was having a good time. By the end of the evening even Dad looked happy. He pulled me to one side as we made our way up to our bedrooms.

'Thanks, mate,' he said quietly.

'No problem.'

I could see he was still nervous deep down. He kept ruffling my hair and he never does that. But he wasn't half as nervous as I was. He and Angela were going to have each other for

company tonight. I was going to have something else. It was following me up the stairs right this moment.

To add to my troubles, the itching was growing worse and I was finding it hard to breathe through my nose. It was like my nostrils were closing up.

Dad ruffled my hair yet again.

'We'll have a wander round Totnes tomorrow, OK?'

'OK.'

'Night, Stevie.'

'Night, Dad.'

'Night, Stevie,' said Angela.

I saw an anxious look from Dad.

'Night, Angela,' I said.

I stood outside my door. They stood outside theirs. I had a feeling there was something else I was supposed to say. I bit my lip.

'Thanks for today,' I muttered. 'All the presents and stuff. And the cake.'

'We'll change the CDs,' said Angela hurriedly.

I opened the door and felt the icy presence brush past into my room. I felt sure Angela noticed me shiver. She opened her mouth to speak but I cut her off.

'It's OK,' I said. 'About the CDs.'

'We'll sort it out,' she said.

'Yeah, well.' I shrugged. 'See you in the morning.'

I dived into my room, closed the door behind me and switched on the light. Something was here with me, something I could not see. I looked quickly about me.

Then I heard a sound in the far corner of the room.

4

SHADOW SOUNDS

Breathing.

It was unmistakable. Yet this was no human being.

It sounded like the breathing of a dog.

I could hear it clearly now that the house was quiet – a low, panting from somewhere by the wardrobe. I glanced towards it. Yet there was no sign of this ghostly animal.

The sound faded away.

That disturbed me even more. At least when I could hear the breathing, I knew roughly where the thing was. I glanced warily about the room.

Nothing.

The itching on my skin was almost unbearable now. I pulled out the bell from under my shirt

and rested it on the armchair by the bed, then rolled up my sleeve to scratch myself.

To my horror, there were sores all over my forearm.

I stared at them. They weren't large but they hadn't been there before and the sight of them filled me with dread.

My breathing was growing worse too. The blockage in my nose was now so thick I couldn't inhale through my nostrils. I started to breathe through my mouth, in, out, in, out, until I too was panting like a dog.

I walked slowly towards the bathroom. The unseen creature brushed against my legs as I passed the end of the bed.

'Go away,' I murmured to it. 'Leave me alone.'

But it didn't. I felt it enter the bathroom with me. I switched on the light and stood in front of the mirror.

The face that stared back filled me with loathing. It was clearly my own. But my eyes

were paler, my nose thicker, my brow higher. Why hadn't Dad and Angela noticed this? Or had my face changed in just the last few minutes?

I undid my shirt and forced myself to look.

Sores were creeping all over my body. I felt a rush of panic.

'No!' I shouted.

I buttoned up my shirt, unable to bear the sight of myself any longer.

The panting came again, closer, and now I caught the smell of the animal. I looked quickly round, certain I would see the creature this time.

But there was nothing there.

I turned off the bathroom light, ran to the bed and jumped in with my clothes on. Then I wrapped the duvet tightly around me and switched off the bedroom light.

Darkness fell upon me.

I peeped out over the top of the duvet. The features of the room were dim, but after a while my eyes grew accustomed to the dark and I started to make things out: the wardrobe, the table, the lamp, the armchair.

The panting drew nearer. Then something jumped onto the bed. I held myself rigid. The thing was down by my feet. I could feel the weight of it. Yet I could see nothing there.

I felt the animal move around for a few minutes, then it seemed to settle. I listened to the panting. It was a chilling sound and I wished it would go away. But now there was an even more disturbing sensation.

Something pushing me in the back.

I tried to move away from it but the pressure continued. I wriggled towards the side of the bed. It wasn't the thing at the bottom. I could still feel its weight there. This was something else. It felt as though someone had climbed into the bed and was trying to shove me out.

I threw back the duvet and stood up. Before me was an empty bed. Yet something was there, something other than the dog.

I moved backwards, keeping my eyes fixed on the bed. My legs bumped against the armchair behind me. I sat slowly down. I could feel the broken bell against my thigh and something lumpy underneath me. I took the bell in one hand and reached down with the other.

The lumpy thing was my jacket. I remembered dropping it there when we arrived that afternoon. I pulled it out and wrapped it around me. Then, still clutching the bell, I stared out at the room.

It was changing before my eyes. The wardrobe, the table, the window, the walls – everything was melting away as though a veil had fallen.

I was still huddled on the chair with my coat pulled over me. But these things too were changing. The chair now seemed smaller, harder, more rickety. My coat had turned into a rough, threadbare cloak with holes in the sides.

Before me was a dark space with a bed. But even that had changed. The metal frame, the duvet, the flowery pillow – those things

were gone. It was now a wooden bed with a coarse blanket thrown back, as though someone had just climbed out.

I saw a figure moving round the far side. It was hard to see in the darkness but I locked my eyes onto it, determined not to lose sight of it. The figure stopped by the end of the bed and was joined by a second shadowy form, and then a third, low to the ground.

I stood up, keeping the cloak wrapped around me and the bell hidden from view.

'What do you want?' I said.

There was no answer. But the three forms started to move towards me.

5

FIGURES IN THE NIGHT

I could make them out now: a boy about my age, a small girl about eight, and a dog – a tough, lean terrier. The boy and the girl were wearing rough cloaks and had faces covered in

sores like the old man. The boy put out a hand to keep the girl back, then stepped forward.

'Who are you?' he demanded.

I shuddered. His face was revolting. The darkness made him shadowy but he seemed horribly real. I could even smell his foul breath.

The room seemed real too, yet it was no longer my room at Maudlin Lodge. The walls were higher and there were heavy beams above me which hadn't been there before. I tried to see through the darkness beyond the bed but it was too deep.

'Who are you?' said the boy again.

I heard the danger in his voice.

'Stevie,' I said quickly.

'There was a Stephen in the Bible,' said the boy. 'They stoned him to death.'

The repetition of the old man's words chilled me.

'I'm not Stephen,' I said. 'I'm Stevie.'

'What kind of a name is that?'

I said nothing. The boy ran his eyes over me.

'I don't trust you,' he said. 'You're not one of us.'

I didn't want to be one of them. Whatever these people were, I wanted nothing to do with them. I tried to step to the side but the boy caught me by the arm.

'Let go,' I said.

'Not till you've told me why you're here.'

I saw a wild energy in his sunken eyes and tried not to show my fear. Then the girl stepped forward.

'He is one of us,' she said. 'Look.'

And she held up my hand, exposing the sores. The boy stared down at them, then pushed my cloak back and studied the skin along my forearm.

'You see?' said the girl.

'I still don't trust him,' said the boy. He looked me hard in the face. 'Where have you come from?'

'I don't know.'

'Of course you know. Do you think I'm stupid?'

I didn't know what to say. I knew where I had come from but I had no idea where I was now. I looked round the room, searching again for the Maudlin Lodge that had once been here. But it was gone.

The girl spoke again to her companion.

'Maybe this boy has come to help us find him.'

'Find who?' I said.

But before either of them could answer, the terrier trotted forward and started to nuzzle at my other hand – the one that was holding the bell in the folds of my cloak.

'What's this?' muttered the boy. 'Where did you get that bell?'

The girl reached out to take it. I let her have it. I could feel a fight coming and needed both hands free. I kept my eyes on the boy. He was glowering at me.

'That's his bell,' he said. 'What have you done?'

'I don't know what you mean.'

He thrust me back against the wall.

'You've murdered him.'

'Who?'

'You know who I mean!'

'The old man?'

'You see? You do know who I mean.' The boy had foam round the edges of his mouth. 'You've killed him,' he snarled.

Again, I tried not to show my fear.

'I didn't do anything to him,' I said. 'I just took his bell. He left it behind him and I picked it up.'

The boy spoke through clenched teeth.

'Where did he leave it?'

'At the spring, the well, whatever it is.'

'The Leechwell?'

'If that's what it's called.'

'Where did he go after that?'

'Down one of the lanes.'

'Which one?'

'The one that heads down the hill.'

I heard a gasp from the little girl.

'Who is this man?' I said to the boy.

He didn't answer. Instead he turned and started a hurried conversation with the girl.

'They'll kill him this time,' he said. 'I'll have to go and look for him.'

'But they'll kill you too.'

'He might not have got inside the town.'

'He nearly did last time.'

'I've still got to go and look for him.'

'It's too dangerous.' The girl gripped him by the arm. 'I don't want you to go.'

'What choice do we have?'

'We could tell Father and Mother.'

'That'll be worse. They'll insist on coming too. Then we'll all be in danger.'

The boy looked sharply back at me. The brotherly tone he'd been using with the girl vanished and the tone of suspicion returned.

'What was the old man wearing when you saw him?'

'A kind of long cloak with a hood,' I said.

He glanced back at the girl.

'He must have stolen one of the spare habits.'

'Mother washed two for the monks this morning,' she said. 'I saw them drying. He could easily have got through the South Gate in that disguise. Especially if he went at dusk, just before the curfew.'

I had no idea what they were talking about. Again I tried to see something of the old Maudlin Lodge. I tried to hear sounds from Dad and Angela's room next door. I tried to pick up something of what had been here before.

But everything had changed. My surroundings were different, my clothes were different, my body was different.

I even felt different. My memories were becoming blurred. I could remember Dad and Angela, and Mum, but I couldn't picture their faces. I couldn't picture the house I lived in. I couldn't picture my school.

My world was losing shape.

All I could see was shadowy figures, a shadowy bed, and the vague outline of the walls and ceiling nearest to me. Beyond that, all was darkness.

'Who is this old man?' I said.

'Our grandfather,' answered the girl.

'And who are you?'

'My name is Maria. This is Stephen, my brother.'

'Stephen?' I said.

'Yes,' he answered, and I heard the defiance in his voice.

'But who are you really?' I said.

'Who are we really?' The boy turned to face me again. 'Don't you mean – what are we really?'

He leaned slowly forward.

'We are what you are,' he said. 'We are the dead.'

6

JOINING THE DEAD

I shuddered.

'You're ghosts, then?'

The boy watched me with his strange, shadowy eyes. Then suddenly he pushed his hand towards me.

'Hold my wrist,' he said.

'I don't want to.'

'Do it.'

I placed my hand round the boy's wrist.

'Squeeze it,' he said.

I squeezed. I could feel his sores under my fingers. They revolted me.

'Tighter,' he commanded. 'Feel my pulse.'

I forced myself to squeeze more tightly. The boy's wrist was even colder than mine, so cold it was hard to believe there could be life under the skin. Yet I felt a sharp, almost angry pulse.

'Do ghosts have a heartbeat?' he said.

I didn't answer.

'Do they breathe like I do?' he went on. 'Do they speak? Do they eat and drink?'

I let go of his wrist, unable to bear the feel of it any longer. He watched me with a sneer.

'Don't want to touch me, do you? I don't blame you. I'm repulsive. I know that. Nobody touches me.'

Little Maria reached out and caught her brother by the hand.

'I touch you,' she said quietly.

52

His sore-ravaged face softened for a moment. But it quickly hardened again as he turned his attention back to me.

'You see?' he said. 'We do all the things others do. We even love. And hate.'

I saw his eyes burning into mine.

'You're not dead,' I said. 'Nor is your sister.'

'We're dead,' he replied. 'We've had our funerals. Just like you.'

'But I'm not the same as you.'

'Yes, you are.'

'I'm not. I'm nothing like you. I'm – '

The boy gave a dry laugh.

'Look at yourself.'

But I didn't need to. I could feel what was happening. My body was withering into a hideous deformity. My limbs were contorting. My eyes were narrowing. My skin was prickling with sores.

I was growing colder. I was losing sensation in my fingers and toes. The blockage in my nose was now so thick I couldn't even sniff.

'Can't breathe, can you?' said the boy, watching me. 'The skin's grown over your nostrils. I've got that problem too.'

I stared back at him, terrified of what he was and what I had become.

'I'm...I'm not like you,' I spluttered.

'You are.'

'I'm not! I'm not!'

The boy leaned closer.

'There's nothing you can do about it. You've joined the dead now.'

I glared back, determined to defy him somehow. On an impulse I grabbed the broken bell from the girl.

'Give it back!' snarled the boy.

'No!'

He lunged for it but I twisted my body round and held the bell away from him.

I had no idea why I was doing this. There was nothing to be gained except more trouble. But the sight of this boy and the thought of being like him made me reckless.

The boy lunged again. Then, to my surprise, the girl stepped in front of him.

'Let him keep it,' she said.

Her brother drew back, breathing hard.

'What do you mean?'

'Let him keep it.'

'But it's not his!'

'Maybe he's meant to have it.'

'What for?'

'Maybe he's going to help us.'

'I'm not,' I said firmly.

I felt the terrier rub itself against my leg. I reached down to cuff the animal away, but then pulled my hand back. There was something in the creature's manner that felt friendly. The girl nodded towards the dog.

'You see?' she said.

'I see nothing,' said the boy in a surly voice.

He pulled her to one side and went on in a breathless whisper. I could tell he didn't want me to hear but I had no difficulty picking up his words.

'I can't get into an argument over the bell,' he was saying. 'I've got to go.'

'I'll come with you,' she said.

'No. It's too dangerous. Stay here with Moss.'

He glanced at the dog, who was still rubbing against my leg.

'If I'm not back by dawn, wake Father and tell him what's happened. But don't let him come after me. Get him to tell the monks.' His eyes flickered in my direction. 'And if this boy gives you any trouble, scream and wake the others.'

The girl looked down at the dog.

'I think the boy's safe,' she said. 'Moss likes him.'

'Well, I don't,' said her brother.

'The feeling's mutual,' I retorted.

The boy turned to me again. I squared up to him, determined to show no weakness; and

on another impulse I said, 'You don't need to
worry about me hurting your sister.'

'Why not?'

I could feel another one of my hunches. A big,
powerful hunch. It told me to keep my mouth
shut and stay put.

'Because I'm coming with you,' I said.

The boy snorted.

'You're not!'

'You can't stop
me,' I said.

He looked me up and down.

'Why would you want to come with me?'

I saw the sneer in his pale eyes. Or was it a dare?

'It'll be dangerous,' he said. 'If they see you, they'll kill you. Have you got the courage?'

I clenched my hands round the bell.

'Have you?' I said.

We scowled at each other. I could feel the boy's spirit challenging me just as mine was challenging him. I felt the dog lick my hand. I reached down and stroked his head.

'Good boy, Moss,' I said. 'Good boy.'

The dog licked my hand again. I looked back at the two figures.

'I'm not your enemy,' I said.

I saw a faint smile on Maria's face. But the boy called Stephen wore the same suspicious frown he had had all along. He searched my eyes for a moment. Then, with a shrug of his shoulders, he spun round.

'We must hurry,' he said.

7

THE TWISTING LANE

He led me into the darkness. I followed, still clutching the broken bell. Little Maria was on one side of me, the dog on the other. I kept my eyes on the boy, anxious in case I lost sight of him.

But the darkness was falling back. It was still night and the room was dim but where before all was black, now I could make out shapes. I could see rows of beds with sleeping figures, some old, some young, all disfigured with sores, just like us.

Some moved in their sleep. Some even murmured as we passed.

But none woke.

We reached a large door. The boy eased it open and nodded me through. I stepped past him onto a broad landing. The dog and Maria followed, then the boy slipped through, closed the door softly behind him and led us down some stairs.

I followed, my mind racing. What had I agreed to? What was this boy leading me into? I had spoken out bravely enough but now I was starting to regret it.

We reached the bottom of the stairs and I found myself in a dim hallway with what looked like a main door at the far end.

Moss scampered ahead and sniffed round it.

The boy followed and quietly slid back the bolt. Then he turned and looked at his sister.

'Keep Moss inside,' he whispered. 'Don't let him follow us out.'

'He might help protect you,' she said.

The boy shook his head.

'He's more likely to give us away. Keep him inside.'

Maria said nothing. She was watching her brother's face, and I knew she could see what I could see.

The fear in his eyes.

She leaned forward and kissed him on the brow. Then, to my surprise, she kissed mine too.

'Please come back,' she whispered.

And before either of us could answer, she bent down to the dog and put a restraining arm round him.

'Go,' she said, not looking up.

The boy stared down at her, as though he wanted her to meet his eyes again. But she didn't. He glanced at me, then opened the big door and ushered me through.

I stepped out into the night and heard the door close behind me. As it did so, I felt the last of my memories slip away. I no longer knew who I was or who I had ever been. I knew a name.

Stevie.

I had the feeling it had once been my name. I knew other names too: Mum, Dad, Angela. I had no idea who they belonged to or what those people were like. And there was another name.

Totnes.

That too was a mystery.

All I knew for certain was that my body had become a monstrous thing, and that I was walking into danger.

'Come on,' said the boy, and he set off up a grassy track.

I followed, glancing about me as I walked. The track ran up a hill with fields to our left and orchards to our right.

I looked back at the building we had left behind. It was high and imposing, and it stood out against the night sky. I could see gardens and outhouses and what looked like some kind of chapel, though it was hard to tell in the darkness.

'Don't lag behind,' called the boy.

I looked ahead and saw he was striding on at a brisk pace as though he wanted to leave me behind. I hurriedly caught him up.

'You won't get rid of me that easily,' I said.

He didn't answer and simply pushed on up the track.

'Where are we going?' I asked breathlessly.

'This way,' he answered, and he turned to the right down a narrow lane bordered by high walls.

It looked strangely familiar though I couldn't remember where I'd seen it before. I knew I'd been here. But it felt different, just as I felt different.

Again I wondered who I was.

'I'm Stevie,' I murmured to myself. 'I'm Stevie, I'm Stevie.'

'Be quiet,' muttered the boy. 'You'll give us away.'

He stopped suddenly in a small open space before a gurgling spring. I recognised it, though again my memories were confused.

The boy looked round at me.

'Leave the bell here by the Leechwell.'

'No.'

'Leave it here!'

'No!' I clutched it to me. 'I'm taking it with me.'

'What for?'

'I don't know. I just...feel I need to have it with me.'

The boy scowled, then all of a sudden the anger drained from his eyes and fear returned. He looked away.

'Bring it if you must. But don't let it ring.'

'It won't ring. It's broken.'

The boy looked back at me.

'This is where it gets dangerous,' he said. 'You don't have to come with me if you don't want to.'

'I'm coming,' I said. 'I've made up my mind.'

The boy held my eyes for a few moments.

'All right,' he said eventually. 'But remember, if you see anybody apart from Grandfather, run.'

And he turned without another word and set off towards the twisting lane that led down the hill. I followed warily, searching the darkness for figures. Every shadow now seemed a threat.

We entered the lane and started down it.

8

WATCHERS AT THE GATE

I was growing more and more scared. I was scared of this narrow lane with its high walls on either side. I was scared of the dangers that lay ahead. But most of all I was scared of the things that were happening to me.

My skin was festering. My breathing was laboured. My limbs were growing colder. I was starting to shiver. My mind was in pieces.

I knew nothing – who I was, what I was, where I was.

Even time seemed to be slipping from my grasp. I was in a place I dimly recognised, yet in a century I did not know.

I stumbled on after the boy.

But now even he was slipping away. His body seemed to be fading into the shadows from which he had first come.

'Stephen!' I called.

His body thickened again. He stopped and turned. I walked up to him and stared into his eyes.

'Keep your voice down,' he murmured. 'We're not far from the gate.'

We walked on and before long I saw the end of the lane ahead and the outline of the town wall beyond.

The boy glanced at me.

'I'm praying Grandfather didn't get inside the town before they closed the South Gate

for the night. If he's outside the walls, we might still find him.'

'But you think he's inside the town, don't you?'

'Yes. He's been trying to get in for years. And if he's disguised himself as a monk, he might have managed it this time.' The boy gave a long sigh. 'They'll kill him if they find him. I know they will.'

'But if the disguise got him in,' I said, 'it'll get him out as well when they open the gate again.'

The boy shook his head.

'He doesn't want to get out again. There's only one place he wants to be. And he'd be happy to die there.'

I heard shouts over to the right. They were some distance away and they weren't coming from the town but from somewhere outside the walls.

The boy heard them too and gripped my arm.

'They've got him. I just know they've got him. Come on. We must do what we can.'

We hurried on down the lane. I kept my eyes on the great town wall rising before us just a short distance ahead. There were more shouts over to the right.

'Keep well down,' whispered the boy. 'And get ready to run.'

We crept forward, keeping close to the side of the lane. The boy was so low it was hard for me to see him in the darkness. Again I had the disconcerting feeling that he was fading away. I reached out and touched him on the back.

'What?' he said.

'I just had to touch you.'

'What for?'

'To make sure you're not a ghost.'

'I told you I'm not.' He looked round at me suddenly. 'Are you?'

I looked away.

'I don't know,' I answered.

And that was the truth.

More shouts rang out. We crept to the end of the lane and crouched in the shadows. Before us was the town wall. The boy leaned close again.

'The South Gate's open,' he whispered.

I stared along the wall. A short way down was a large, open gate. Two men were standing outside it, staring towards the source of the shouting. But I could not tell what was causing the commotion. The wall of the lane blocked our view.

The boy whispered again.

'Do what I do. But keep low and don't make a sound.'

I saw him glance towards the two men. Neither seemed to be looking our way but it was hard to be sure in the darkness.

'Now,' he said.

He dashed out from the shadows and across the open space. I raced after him, holding the bell close to my chest. We reached the town wall together and threw ourselves down at the base.

'Did they see us?' I whispered.

'Don't think so,' said the boy.

We studied the watchers at the gate. They were still staring down the slope and seemed unaware of us. And now I could see what was causing the noise.

A crowd of men were busy on the slopes below the town wall. But they weren't killing an old man. They were trying – without much success – to round up some pigs.

The boy turned to me, his eyes dark and grave.

'That's the second time this week the pigs have got out of the town before the gate's closed for the night. It's probably been open for hours while those men try to drive the animals back in. You know what that means?'

'The old man's inside the town.'

The boy nodded.

'Almost certainly.'

He glanced up at the sky.

'Dawn's coming,' he said.

I looked up and saw pale streaks stretching across the eastern horizon.

'Maria will be waking the others soon,' he said. 'I must find Grandfather and get him out somehow. If the others come looking for us, they'll die too.'

I looked back at him. His body was now eerily transparent. He seemed so fragile I felt I could blow him away. Yet his voice was full of strength.

'You'd better leave me now,' he said. 'It's too dangerous for you. If those men see us, they'll call others, and we'll both be killed.'

He touched me on the arm.

'Goodbye.'

I caught hold of his hand as he made to withdraw it.

'No goodbyes,' I said.

'What do you mean?'

'Let's go,' I said.

And I edged towards the gate.

9

PURSUIT

I knew this was reckless. The men were right by the entrance and we would be easier to see now that dawn was on its way. But some of the darkness still lingered and after a few cautious steps we found ourselves close to the gate.

Still the men hadn't turned in our direction. They were staring down the slope and chuckling at the pandemonium below. I watched nervously, trying to will them to move away from the entrance.

A dog barked somewhere to the right. Somehow I just knew it was Moss. I looked quickly round at the boy. He nodded, frowning. I turned towards the lane we had just come down. There was no sign of the dog yet, but he'd be here soon and he'd give us away for sure. He'd run straight up to us.

But the bark had stirred the men too. They took a few steps away from the entrance, their eyes on the lane.

I felt the boy push me in the back but I needed no prompting. I darted through the gate and raced into the town, the boy close beside me. To my horror, I heard shouts break out behind us.

'You there!'

'Stop!'

'They've seen us,' I muttered.

'Keep running,' said the boy.

'Which way?'

'Follow me!'

I saw plots of land stretching towards a line of houses in the centre of the town. The boy was tearing across the nearest of these towards a woodpile in the middle.

I pelted after him, gripping the bell as tightly as I could.

More shouts rang out behind us, this time from several voices.

'Over there!'

'Where?'

'Heading for the woodpile!'

'Come on!'

Fear gripped me. We had no chance now. They'd close the South Gate and hunt us down. We reached the woodpile, ran round the back and threw ourselves to the ground.

The boy's face was white with terror.

'Is there anything we can do?' I said.

He shook his head.

'Stay alive as long as we can. But it won't be for long. Not now we've been seen.'

We stared at each other in silence.

'What are we going to do?' I said.

The boy clenched his fists.

'I'm going to find Grandfather. I can at least say goodbye to him.'

'But you don't know where he is.'

'Yes, I do.'

We peered round the side of the woodpile. A group of men was forming – the two from the gate and five or six more. I could hear an angry murmur from them as they started across the plot towards us.

'Come on,' said the boy.

And we dashed towards the houses in the centre of the town.

'There!' came a shout.

I didn't look back. I just ran. I knew the men were faster than we were but we had a head

start and there was just a chance we'd reach the houses first.

The buildings were all dark and so far silent, but I knew this wouldn't last. The men would gather up a mob and rouse the town in no time.

I was growing tired already. Somewhere in my memory I remembered a boy who was strong, a boy who could run and fight. But now I felt like a shadow.

And the boy in front of me was becoming one. As light fell upon him, he was fading again from view. I saw him still but only just.

I gripped the bell more tightly than ever. I didn't know why I was still clinging to it. I just felt I had to. We reached the houses and darted between them into the main street of the town.

'Head for St Mary's Church!' hissed the boy. 'We might just get there before they see where we went.'

We hurtled down the main street. But even as we ran, I heard the sound of voices inside the houses. The shouts of the men were loud and close and the town was waking up.

'Hurry!' said the boy.

I was exhausted now. My legs were shaking. The bell felt heavy. I drove myself on after the boy. But he too was growing weak. I could see it in his faltering steps; and he had almost faded from view.

The church appeared at last.

'This way!' called the boy.

He ran round the outer wall and stopped at a large iron gate.

'Please don't be locked,' he murmured. 'Please don't be locked.'

It wasn't locked. The boy pulled it open, pushed me through and closed it after us.

We were in the graveyard.

'Keep out of sight of the gate,' he whispered. 'They might not have seen us go in.'

We moved to the side, keeping close to the wall that ran along the main street of the town. Before us was the silent church, its high stone tower thrusting up into the brightening sky. Next to it, within the walled enclosure, was the ancient priory, silent in the early dawn.

I looked back at the boy. He was just an airy form now, though his face was still clear.

'You told me you weren't a ghost,' I said. 'You promised.'

He didn't answer. He was staring over the graveyard with tears in his eyes.

'He's not here,' he said.

No one was here. We were alone.

But I knew it would not be for long. I could hear shouts in the main street – loud, angry, dangerous shouts. And they were drawing closer.

10

THE RETURN
OF THE SOLDIER

The boy turned towards me. He was barely visible now.

'You're fading,' he said suddenly. 'You're disappearing.'

'But....' I stared at him. 'You're the one who's fading.'

'Maybe neither of us is real.'

He leaned closer.

'Who are you?' he said. 'Where have you come from?'

I didn't know. I was in another body, another mind, another time. Another Totnes, even.

I said nothing. I could not speak.

More shouts came from the other side of the wall. I could tell from the sound that the

number of people had swelled. It was a crowd now.

I clutched the bell tightly to my chest.

'I thought Grandfather would be here,' said the boy.

'Why?' I asked.

More light stretched across the eastern sky.

The boy walked to the centre of the graveyard and stopped. He was a spectral figure now, just as I seemed to be to him. I walked over and joined him. He was standing on one of the little mounds. It had a tiny, wooden cross that had long been broken.

'She's buried somewhere here,' he said. 'We don't know which grave. He's never been told. He's never been allowed into the town, not even to stand in the graveyard and pay his respects to her, wherever she lies.'

The boy looked down.

'Maybe it's the grave we're standing on now. It's as good a one as any to choose.'

The shouts on the other side of the wall were growing louder. No faces had appeared at the gate yet. But it was only a matter of time before someone saw us.

I placed the bell gently on the grave, then straightened up and looked for the boy.

He was almost gone. I could just make out his eyes and the blurry outline of his body and head.

'Her name was Isabella,' he said. 'Grandfather married her when he was a healthy young man. They had a son, who later became my father.

Then Grandfather went away to France to fight for the old King.'

The boy threw a look of contempt towards the hidden mob on the other side of the wall.

'He wasn't like those cowards. He was a hero. He fought at the scene of the King's greatest triumph.'

For a moment the boy's body seemed to return. But it quickly faded again. He glanced towards the gate, then went on.

'He was badly wounded during the battle. He got separated from the King's men and cut down, and left for dead. But some peasants found him and cared for him. He survived and two years later he was strong enough to

return to England. But by then the disease had taken him over.'

More shouts rang out from the street.

I saw the boy's ghostly arms reach out towards me.

'Where are you?' he whispered. 'I can't see you any more.'

I reached out my own arms and pulled him close. He had slipped from view now. Yet I could feel his body, even the sores on his skin. He was shaking as I was.

I knew the rest of the story. I didn't know how. I just knew it all. But the boy finished it anyway.

'He reached Totnes and found himself an outcast. Isabella had died in his absence and his son was kept from him for fear of infection. But the young boy ran away and joined him, and became infected too. And the infected boy later married an infected girl and they had two children, first myself and then Maria. We were clean in the beginning. Then the disease claimed us too.'

I pulled him closer.

'I'm scared,' he whispered.

'So am I.'

The first of the faces appeared in the gate. It was followed at once by a shout.

'The graveyard!'

The shout was taken up by other voices all along the street.

'The graveyard!'

'The graveyard!'

I felt the boy shudder. And I shuddered too.

The gate swung open and the mob poured in. But they didn't come straight for us. They spread out around the wall, keeping back but blocking the way out.

I held on to the boy and looked round at them. There were about thirty, mostly men but some women too, their faces hard with loathing.

All were carrying stones.

But before they could throw them, the gate opened again and a new figure appeared. I

heard a gasp from the crowd and they drew back.

It was the old man.

He walked slowly towards me. Behind him I saw the mob re-form to block the gate. But the old man didn't look back. He stopped in front of me.

'Why haven't they come for us?' I said.

'Because they're frightened too,' he answered. 'That's what makes them dangerous.'

I looked for the boy I had been holding. He was no longer there. I couldn't even feel him in my arms. I stared back at the old man.

He was watching me with a weary smile on his ravaged face.

'It's kind of you to bring back my bell, Stephen,' he said. 'But you appear to have forgotten your own.'

I picked it up and held it out to him.

'It's broken,' I said.

'No, it's not,' said the old man. 'It's just crusted with earth on the inside. I was trying to wash it out at the Leechwell but I got interrupted and then walked off and forgot about it. You've still got your fingers. Scrape out the earth for me, there's a good boy.'

I scraped at the earth until the inside of the bell was almost clear.

'That'll do,' said the old man.

He took the bell and clasped it somehow in one of his fingerless hands. Then he turned to the mob and shook it. A cracked ringing resounded over the graveyard.

The response was a terrifying roar from the crowd.

The old man stopped ringing and put a hand on my shoulder.

'It's going to be unpleasant, Stephen,' he said. 'I'm so sorry I've brought this upon you.

You didn't bring little Maria with you, I hope?'

'No, Grandfather.'

'Good.'

I hesitated.

'Did you pay your respects to Isabella?'

'Yes, my boy. She and I have said our goodbyes. And now you and I must do the same.'

He pulled me close and held me.

'Be brave, Stephen,' he said. 'Braver than you've ever been.'

And he turned back to the mob.

11

FACING THE MOB

They were moving towards us. I felt Grandfather's arm on my shoulder. He took a step forward and I stepped with him.

The crowd stopped, then edged back. They weren't going to let us go; that was clear. But they weren't going to get too close to us either.

I sensed Grandfather standing proud and erect beside me. But my eyes were on the mob. They were a sea of faces. Yet all I saw was one thing.

Hatred.

And all I heard was one word.

'Lepers!'

It went whispering round the graveyard like a curse.

'Lepers!'

'Lepers!'

'Lepers!'

The first of the stones came flying through the air.

I ducked but Grandfather didn't move. It shot past his head and crashed against the wall behind us. But it stirred up the mob. If they had been timid before, they burst into activity now. A cloud of stones and small rocks whistled towards us.

Three or four thudded into my chest. I slipped from Grandfather's grasp and fell to the ground, pain throbbing around my ribs. Somehow I scrambled back to my feet. Grandfather was doubled over in pain. He was still clutching the bell but he had been badly hit.

More stones came flying. None hit me but several smashed into Grandfather's face. He fell backwards across the unknown grave. I ran over to him and knelt down.

'Grandfather!'

The mob roared in triumph, then suddenly I heard new shouts.

'Stop!'

'Stop!'

I felt a surge of hope and looked up. Monks were hurrying out from the priory to break up the stoning. But it was no good. The anger of

the mob was too great and men were already forcing the monks back.

I heard more shouts, this time from the street.

'Let them go!'

For a moment the gate swung open and I saw men trying to push through – more monks and some of the townsfolk, calling for the stoning to be stopped. Again the mob forced them back. As the gate closed once more, I saw something small shoot through the gap.

'Moss!' I shouted. 'Here, boy!'

The dog ran forward and rubbed itself against my hand. I leaned closer to the old man. His face was bloody. His eyes were dim. His breathing was jerky.

'Grandfather,' I murmured. 'Don't die.'

He stared up at me.

'Don't show them you're afraid, Stephen.'

The dog licked the old man's face.

I heard more shouts of protest from the monks and the townsfolk in the street. But the baying of the mob was louder.

'Lepers!' came the chant. 'Lepers! Lepers! Lepers!'

And more chants.

'Sinners!'

'Filth!'

'Living dead!'

More stones came flying through the air.

Two hit me in the side of the face and knocked me down. I rolled over the ground, moaning. Somewhere nearby I heard Moss yelping with pain. I dragged myself to my feet again and saw the terrier hobbling on three legs.

Grandfather was motionless. His eyes were glazed. Blood was dribbling from his temple.

'Lepers!' came the shouts.

'Filth!'

'Filth!'

'Filth!'

I crawled over the grass towards the old man.
He had dropped his bell and it had rolled to the
side of him. I picked it up and crawled over to
him. He was still breathing but I knew there
was no hope.

'Grandfather,' I said softly.

He didn't speak.

'Grandfather, please don't die.'

More stones were falling upon us. Yet the old
man looked almost mildly up at them.

'Our arrows fell more thickly than this,' he
murmured, 'on the field of Agincourt.'

I saw the life fade from his eyes.

And I knew he was gone.

Moss hobbled forward and sniffed his master's face, then turned away and gave a howl. There was a cheer from the mob.

I stood up, gripping the bell tightly in my hand, and faced them. I saw arms swing back, ready to hurl more stones. But before they could do so, I strode forward.

They drew back at once and I heard whispers of alarm.

I stopped and glowered at them.

'Filth!' shouted one, a farmer with a pitchfork in one hand and a clutch of stones in the other.

'Sinner!' screamed a woman. 'This is holy ground!'

A roar of agreement ran round the mob. I shook the bell with all the fury in my heart. It clanged its demented song into the chilly dawn.

'Filth,' whispered the mob. 'Living dead.'

I took another step towards them. They moved back as one body.

'Yes!' I yelled, watching them. 'You mustn't come near, must you? You might end up like me!'

I threw the bell across the churchyard and ripped off my shirt.

A murmur of disgust ran round the crowd. I saw monks trying to push through again from the priory. I saw men in the street struggling to open the gate again. Even the vicar of St Mary's was there, protesting.

But none could get past the mob.

I no longer cared. I thought of Grandfather lying dead behind me. I thought of his words: 'Don't show them you're afraid'.

I glared at the faces before me.

'You call us lepers!' I spat. 'You call us filth! You call us living dead!'

I scratched at my sores until the blood flowed from them.

'We're human beings!' I screamed.

I saw eyes filled with revulsion. I screamed at them again.

'Is there any one of you less ugly than me?'

No one answered.

'Is there?' I screamed. 'Is there?'

I ran back to Grandfather's body and knelt down. Out of the corner of my eye I saw the mob edge forward again.

I took no notice of them now, nor the monks trying to push through the mob, nor the worthies from the town trying to break through the gate. It would make no difference now.

I bent down and kissed Grandfather's cheek. Then I stood over him and waited. I felt Moss rub himself against my leg. But I did not look down at him. I looked instead for the stone that would kill me.

It came from the right. I saw a burly arm whip through the air. I saw a heavy globe spinning towards my face. It struck me on the spot where little Maria had kissed me.

As I fell to the ground, I was sure I felt her kiss me again.

12

THROUGH THE VORTEX

I remember darkness whirling about me. I remember twisting through space, twisting through time, twisting through terror. I remember panic and pain and helplessness. I remember all feeling going – and then coming back again.

I remember light blinding me and water gurgling over me, hands tearing at my skin, and then a voice calling out.

'Stevie! Stop! You'll hurt yourself!'

I gave a start and looked up to see Angela's worried face staring down at me. Behind her was the heavy globe that had struck me down. It was spinning towards my face again.

'No!' I shouted and put my hands up to cover myself.

But it was only the sun.

'Easy,' said Angela. 'It's just the dawn coming.'

I stared at her in confusion, then suddenly realised where I was.

I was sprawled in one of the baths of the Leechwell, the same one the old man had been in that first time I saw him. I was fully clothed and I was soaked through from the water trickling out of the little spout.

I started to run my hands over my body, feeling the skin on my arms, my legs, my neck, my face. There were no sores or blemishes of any kind. I stood up and walked over to Angela. She was watching me anxiously.

'What's happened, Stevie? You were lying there under the water with your eyes closed. And you were scratching yourself like you wanted to tear your skin off.'

'I did want to tear my skin off.'

'Well, you shouldn't. You've got lovely skin.' She shook her head. 'You're so lucky. I've got terrible skin. I've been embarrassed about it ever since I was a girl.'

I thought of Stephen and Maria, and the old man.

'You've got nice skin,' I said eventually.

'I don't think so, Stevie. But it's kind of you to say so.'

'Dad doesn't seem to have a problem with it.'

She smiled.

'I suppose he doesn't. And talking of your dad, I'd better ring him. He's been worried sick about you.'

She pulled out her mobile and was soon speaking to Dad.

'He's fine. Just a bit wet. Where are you?' A pause, then, 'OK. See you back at Maudlin Lodge.'

I climbed out of the Leechwell and stood there in my sodden clothes.

'Is he mad at me?' I said.

'More worried than mad. What's going on, Stevie?'

'I don't know. It's like…'

But I couldn't find the words to describe my experience. And I wasn't sure I wanted to.

We made our way back towards Maudlin Lodge.

'How did you find out I was missing?' I said.

'It was your dad,' said Angela. 'He woke up in the night and remembered he'd left his glasses in the dining room. So he went out to the landing and was about to go downstairs when he noticed your door was open. He looked inside and saw you weren't there. We've spent the whole night looking for you.'

'He'll kill me,' I murmured.

'No, he won't. He'll just be glad to see you safe.'

And to my relief she was right. Dad was waiting for us outside Maudlin Lodge and he didn't scream at me at all. He just held me.

'I'm sorry, Dad,' I said. 'I'm really sorry.'

'You're not hurt, Stevie? Tell me you're not hurt.'

'I'm not hurt, Dad.'

'Come inside the house.'

We went in.

'Go up and change into some dry clothes,' said Dad. 'Then meet us in the lounge. We'll be more comfortable there.'

I felt nervous entering my bedroom again. But it was just as it had been when we first arrived.

I went into the bathroom and took off my clothes, then stood in front of the mirror.

The boy who looked back was the Stevie I had always known. My skin was normal. My breathing was normal.

And yet nothing was normal. I felt different. And I was still scared.

I towelled myself down, put on dry clothes and went downstairs to join Dad and Angela in the lounge. It was a big, comfortable room I hadn't been in before with ornaments in glass cases and a pleasant air of peace.

But I felt no peace in myself. I slumped into an armchair, desperate to be left alone so that I could try to make some sense of what had happened to me.

'You don't need to explain anything, Stevie,' said Dad. 'Not if you don't want to. All I need to know is that you're OK. And that you didn't get into any trouble.'

'I'm OK,' I said. 'And I didn't get into any trouble.'

Both lies but I could think of no other answer.

I heard footsteps outside the room and looked up. A woman was standing in the doorway, smiling at me.

'Morning, Stevie,' she said.

'Morning,' I answered, wondering who she was.

Dad glanced up at her.

'Sorry about all the running around last night,' he said. 'Hope we didn't disturb you too much.'

'Not a problem,' said the woman. 'Is everything all right?'

'Everything's fine.'

'Good. Anybody want some tea?'

'That would be lovely. Thank you, Mrs Capstick.'

I stared at her. Mrs Capstick? This woman seemed nothing like the batty creature I remembered from yesterday.

'Mrs Capstick?' I said.

'Yes, Stevie?'

'Are you...I mean...is there another Mrs Capstick living here?'

'Not unless my husband's got another wife he hasn't told me about.'

At which point a man appeared at her shoulder.

'Talking about me again?' he said. 'What have I done now?'

'Nothing,' she retorted. 'As usual. Go and make these good people some tea.'

The man looked at her good-naturedly, then gave me a wink.

'All right, Stevie?'

I stared at him. He seemed as unfamiliar to me as the woman. Yet there was no doubting who they were. I didn't answer. I couldn't speak.

It didn't seem to matter. The man simply gave me another wink, then turned and headed for the kitchen, followed by his wife.

I looked away, more bewildered than ever. Nothing made sense any more. I felt safe in this tranquil room. Yet even here I could feel a deep, overwhelming sadness.

The tea came in and we drank it in silence. Then Dad stood up.

'I can see you need a bit of time to yourself, Stevie. Am I right?'

'Yes.'

'Thought so. I know the signs.' He smiled down at me. 'See you later for breakfast. We'll be in our room if you need us.'

They closed the door quietly after them – and at once I was crying.

I cried for myself. I cried for Dad and Angela. I cried for Mum. But most of all I cried for Stephen, and little Maria.

And a brave old man, and the wife he grieved for.

And ultimately died for.

It was some time before the tears stopped. When they did, I realised someone was standing in the doorway again.

It was Mrs Capstick. She had a vase of flowers under one arm and a girl of about eight holding onto her free hand.

'This is my daughter Maria,' she said.

I felt a stab of pain. But I managed to speak.

'Hello, Maria.'

The little girl didn't answer.

'Don't worry if she's quiet,' said Mrs Capstick.

'I've told her your name and said what a friendly boy you are. But she's shy of strangers.'

Mrs Capstick ran her eye over the room.

'I was just wondering where to put these flowers. How about on top of that cabinet in the far corner?'

I turned and looked towards the other end of the room. And felt a shiver pass through me.

On top of the cabinet was a bell.

13

BACK TO THE WELL

I stood up and walked over to it. Then, after a long hesitation, I picked it up.

There was no question about it. This was the old man's bell. And everything was intact. It would ring if I shook it. But I did not dare.

I put it back on the cabinet and found my hand was shaking.

'It's supposed to be a leper's bell,' said Mrs Capstick. 'There used to be a leper hospital somewhere round here.'

She walked up to me, with Maria close beside her, and placed the flowers next to the bell.

'The building was outside the town walls,' she said. 'That's because lepers had to be kept in isolation. They weren't allowed into Totnes and if they left the hospital to go anywhere, they

had to ring a bell to warn healthy people to keep clear.'

I looked uneasily around me, images from the past floating into my mind.

'When was it built?' I murmured. 'This leper hospital.'

Mrs Capstick pulled a book from a nearby shelf, searched for a page, then started to read aloud:

The leper hospital of St Mary Magdalene was known as the Maudlin. It's thought to have been built around the end of the twelfth century. It was a large building with its own chapel, gardens and orchards and it was situated outside the town walls to the east of the Leechwell. It was run by monks from the priory in Totnes. Neither the Maudlin nor the priory buildings exist today.

More images floated into my mind. And I shivered again.

Mrs Capstick looked up from the book.

'Are you all right?' she said. 'You've gone pale. Shall I get your mum?'

'She's not my – ' I began, then stopped. Somehow it no longer mattered who Angela was and who she wasn't. I hardly knew who I was any more.

'You don't need to get my mum,' I said. I took a slow breath. 'Where did you get the bell?'

'From the previous owner of the house. He didn't want to keep it. Said it freaked him out. He told me it dates back to the time of Agincourt.'

'Agincourt!' I said.

The old man had spoken that name as he lay dying. Mrs Capstick saw the confusion on my face.

'You must know about Agincourt,' she said.

'I...I'm not sure exactly what...'

'It was a famous battle,' she said. 'King Henry V won a great victory over the French in 1415, largely thanks to the skill of the English archers.'

I tried to think. The old man had been wounded at Agincourt. Yet he would have been a young man in 1415. So when had he died in the churchyard?

Thirty or forty years later, I supposed. Some time around 1450.

But the date hardly mattered. What mattered was that he should have lived. And so should the boy who died with him.

Mrs Capstick handed me the book, still open at the page.

'Here,' she said. 'You might find it interesting.' She took a bloom from the vase. 'And give this to your mum. She's nice.'

'Thank you,' I said, taking it.

'Come on, Maria.'

And they left the room.

I looked down at the book. Somehow it scared me, just as the bell scared me. I made myself read on from the point where Mrs Capstick had stopped:

Leprosy is a terrifying disease. It rots bone, nerves and flesh and creates dreadful deformities. Throughout history its victims have had to suffer not just the ravages of the disease but the prejudice and persecution of others.

The disease came to be known as 'the living death'. Victims were treated as though they had already died. They were given funerals and pronounced 'dead to society'.

It is impossible to imagine the suffering they must have undergone.

But I could imagine it. I had walked with the dead. And I had died with them.

Dad and Angela came back in.

'Breakfast,' said Dad. 'Then a walk into Totnes.'

I held out the flower to Angela.

'For you,' I said.

'Thank you, Stevie.' She kissed me on the cheek and took it. 'What's the book?'

I handed it to her without a word. She read in silence for a while, then looked up.

'You remember the place where I found you? Listen to this.'

She started to read aloud:

The Leechwell is one of the most mysterious sites in Totnes. Its waters are thought by many to have healing properties. There is a legend that lepers from the Maudlin used to walk from the Leechwell down the ancient walled lane to worship at St Mary's Church. But this cannot be true. Lepers would never have been allowed into the town. Such was the terror their presence caused they would almost certainly have been stoned to death.

I saw the faces in the churchyard again. I saw the fists, the stones, the spinning globe. I saw the ground rushing up to meet me.

I ate my breakfast in silence, then made my way upstairs to fetch my coat and rucksack for the walk into Totnes. I was in another world now. I couldn't think. I couldn't feel.

I could only remember.

I found Dad and Angela waiting in the hall with Mr and Mrs Capstick. I tried to smile but it was no good. My features were frozen. I heard a sound behind me and turned. Maria was watching me from the top of the stairs.

'Goodbye, Stephen,' she called.

Dad gave her a friendly grin.

'He likes to be called Stevie, sweetheart.'

I looked quickly round at him.

'Stephen's OK.' I said.

'What?'

'Stephen's OK.'

Dad stared at me.

'You serious?'

'Yeah.'

I caught Maria's eye and managed a smile at last.

'See you later,' I said.

And she smiled back.

Dad put an arm round me.

'Ready to go...Stephen?'

'Just one thing.'

I'd felt another hunch. A really important one. And for once I wasn't going to ignore it.

I ran into the lounge, took another bloom from the vase and placed it inside my rucksack. Then I ran back to the others.

'OK,' I said.

We set off up the hill. I had already decided which way I wanted to go into Totnes and I was ready to argue with Dad if he had other ideas. But it was clear he had the same intentions as me.

'I've got to see this Leechwell,' he said. 'Everyone else seems to know about it except me.'

We started down the little alleyway and I soon heard the trickle of water. It was a restful sound, a sound I needed to hear. A few moments later we were standing before the spring where I had first seen the old man.

There was no one here now but us.

Yet it was strange. As I stood there with Dad and Angela, I felt sure there were presences around us. They weren't spooky. They were just sad.

'Amazing place,' said Dad. 'And which way is it from here into Totnes?'

I nodded towards the walled lane that twisted away down the slope.

'Ready to walk on?' he said.

'You two go ahead. I'll catch you up.'

'Are you sure you...?'

He studied my face for a moment, then answered his own question.

'No, you're fine.' He patted me on the shoulder. 'You're fine.'

And he and Angela set off down the lane.

I waited till they'd disappeared from view, then turned back to the Leechwell. It looked so beautiful in the morning sunlight. I climbed down into the nearest of the stone baths.

Water gurgled over my feet but I walked on to the far wall with the open grate. The ledge was still covered with the ornaments that had been there before. The love-heart with the words written on it was in exactly the same place. It was like standing in a little shrine.

I stared down at the running water.

'So are you a healing spring?' I murmured. 'Can you make the dead well again?'

The water sounded strangely musical as it washed over my feet.

I reached inside my rucksack, took out the flower and placed it on the ledge. Then I closed my eyes.

I didn't see darkness. I saw misty faces, misty forms.

I whispered to them.

'I won't forget.'

I heard a whimpering sound and opened my eyes.

There was no one to be seen. Yet I knew what the whimpering was. I climbed out of the Leechwell and stood there for a moment. Then something brushed against my legs. I looked down at the empty space and heard the whimpering again.

'I won't forget,' I whispered. 'I promise I won't forget.'

And I set off down the lane towards Totnes.